Down the Chimney
with Googol and Googolplex

Nelly Kazenbroot

W9-ASK-800

ORCA BOOK PUBLISHERS

Library and Archives Canada Cataloguing in Publication
Kazenbroot, Nelly, 1960–
Down the chimney with Googol and Googolplex / Nelly Kazenbroot.
(Orca echoes)

ISBN 10: 1-55143-290-0 / ISBN 13: 978-1-55143-290-8

I. Title. II. Series.
PS8571.A965D69 2004   jc813'.54   C2004-900640-1

First published in the United States, 2004
Library of Congress Control Number: 2004100823

Summary: What are two little alien robots and their new friends Pippa and Troy
to do when the neighborhood bully tries to interfere with their scavenger hunt?

Orca Book Publishers gratefully acknowledges the support for its publishing programs
provided by the following agencies: the Government of Canada through the Canada
Book Fund and the Canada Council for the Arts, and the Province of British
Columbia through the BC Arts Council and the Book Publishing Tax Credit.

MIX
Paper from
responsible sources
FSC® C103214

*Orca Book Publishers is dedicated to preserving the environment and
has printed this book on Forest Stewardship Council® certified paper.*

Design by Lynn O'Rourke

ORCA BOOK PUBLISHERS
www.orcabook.com

Printed and bound in Canada.

18 17 16 15 • 6 5 4 3

To my husband, Stephen,
and our two space aliens,
Izabel and Sebastian.
—N.K.

Chapter One
Scavenger Hunt

Googol and Googolplex have circled the earth three times in their spaceship. They come from a place with lots of corners and edges and the round earth confuses them. There seems to be no end or beginning to it.

"We must land," Googol tells Googolplex.

"Yes. But where?" Googolplex asks.

Googolplex spins his head around three times as he looks out all the windows of their spaceship.

"How about on top of that big red house?" Googolplex says.

It is a very nice house with lots of square windows and a triangular roof.

"Perfect," Googol answers. He steers their spaceship towards the house and lands on the peak of the roof.

"Perfect," says Googolplex. He rolls out of the spaceship on his super-retractable self-adhesive wheels. Then he rolls right along the peak of the roof until he is next to the chimney. "This must be the back door."

Googol pulls himself up on top of the chimney and stares down the square hole. It is just the right shape and size for a square-headed robot.

"Perfect," says Googol. "Let's go in."

At the other end of the chimney is the Sinclairs' family room. Pippa and Troy Sinclair are sitting in this room, arguing about which show they should watch on TV. Pippa is five and she likes to watch cartoons. Troy is eight and he likes to watch cooking shows and sports. It is difficult for them to agree on a show. But it is not difficult for them to agree that they can hear something coming down their chimney.

Googol and Googolplex roll out of the fireplace onto the carpet. The corners of their square red heads, square blue shoulders and triangular yellow toes are covered in soot.

Pippa claps her hands together. "Santa's helpers!"

"Don't be silly, Pippa. It's not Christmastime," Troy tells her. "They're Martians!"

Googol's head spins around three times, and Googolplex bleeps and blurps noisily.

"We are not Martians! We are Googol and Googolplex," Googol says.

"We are looking for snow," Googolplex says.

Pippa and Troy look at each other. "Snow!"

"It's almost summer!" Troy says. "There's no snow around here at this time of year!"

"Oh, dear." Googol gives three sad beeps.

"Dear me," Googolplex says. "Maybe this list of ours isn't going to be so easy to fill, after all."

"What list?" Troy asks.

There is a whirring sound inside of Googolplex. A bunch of lights flash on his stomach, and then a long piece of paper slides out of his mouth.

Troy grabs this list and begins to read it.

"Six snowballs, four sand dollars, a tutu, the song of a blackbird, two peacock feathers, a chocolate bar, all the colors of the rainbow…"

Troy shakes his head and stops reading the list. "This is going to be a very hard list to fill."

Pippa reaches into the pocket of her overalls and pulls out a chocolate bar. "You can have my chocolate bar. That'll be a start."

"Thank you, ugly human," Googol says. "But a robot always starts at the beginning of his list and goes to the end."

"If you're going to be picky about it, you won't get anywhere!" Troy tells them.

"What do you mean 'ugly'?" Pippa asks, frowning.

Googolplex and Googol look at each other then back at Pippa and Troy.

"All humans are ugly," Googol says.

"They have soft bumpy bodies with messy hairs all over the place," Googolplex says.

"They have wet mouths and waxy ears," Googol says.

"And there's not one nice sharp edge or corner on their whole bodies!"

Troy runs a hand through his messy red hair. Pippa sucks in her wet lips.

"Well, so what! That doesn't mean you can call us ugly. My name is Troy and this is Pippa."

Pippa holds out her chocolate bar to Googol for the second time. Googol's pale blue eyes glow warmly as he takes the bar from her. She smiles back at him.

"Now, where are we going to find six snowballs?" Googolplex asks.

"At the North Pole, of course!" Pippa says.

"Will you take us there?" Googol asks.

Troy laughs. "The North Pole is a long way from here."

"Our spaceship is very fast!" Googol says.

Troy's eyes light up. "You have a spaceship?"

"It's on the roof of your house," Googolplex says.

Troy looks at Pippa. "We could go with them to the North Pole if they promise to have us back before dinner."

"I suppose so," Pippa says, though she is not as sure about this as her brother.

"Shouldn't you ask your king for permission first?" Googol asks.

Pippa and Troy laugh.

"We don't have a king," Pippa says, "just a father."

"And he always works in the study until dinner-time," Troy says.

"Perfect," Googolplex says. "We'll make sure we're back by dinnertime."

Googol and Googolplex stand back to let Troy and Pippa lead the way out of the house. "After you, ugly humans."

Troy and Pippa roll their eyes. Then they stuff their snowsuits and boots into a bag and keep right on going.

Chapter Two
An Invisible Spaceship

Troy and Pippa stand beside the robots and look up at the roof of their house.

"I don't see a spaceship," Troy says.

"No, you wouldn't," Googolplex says. "It is invisible to humans."

"I'll bring it down," Googol says. He tips sideways and begins to roll right up the side of the house.

Pippa's mouth hangs open. "Gee, I wish I could do that."

"That is impossible. You do not have super-retractable self-adhesive wheels on your feet," Googolplex says.

Googol disappears when he steps into the spaceship. Pippa and Troy don't see him again until he steps out beside them on their front lawn. The spaceship is hardly any noisier than a buzzing bee.

"Cool!" Troy says.

Googol hands Pippa and Troy each a pair of green glasses. When they put these on they can see the spaceship. It is just like the robots—red and blue and yellow with lots of flashing lights and nice sharp edges.

"Come along! Up you go."

Once Pippa and Troy have climbed the ramp into the spaceship, Googol takes the green glasses back.

"You won't need these now," Googol says.

And he's right. Pippa and Troy can see the inside of the spaceship just fine.

"This is so weird!" Troy says. "Where did you guys come from, anyway?"

"A Sunship," Googolplex says.

"There are Sunships throughout the universe," Googolplex explains. "For many, many years they will stay in one spot."

"Then, suddenly, they shoot across to a new place," Googol says.

"Like a shooting star?" Pippa asks.

Googol's head spins around three times. "Exactly."

"Since our Sunship has just arrived in your solar system," Googolplex says, "we have been sent on a scavenger hunt…"

"…to learn about the new planets around us," Googol says.

"Well, the first thing you'd better find," Troy says, "is a couple of chairs."

Pippa looks around her at the empty floor of the spaceship. "Yes, what are we suppose to sit on—our heads?"

"Oh, dear, that would be most uncomfortable!" Googol says.

Googolplex pushes a button on the wall and two little seats with cushions flip down. "Would you not rather use these?"

Troy and Pippa laugh and take their seats. Once they have fastened their seat belts, the robots snap themselves into the cockpit and start up the spaceship. In an instant, they are high up in the sky and flying past the land towards the ocean.

Googolplex stares down at the whitecaps foaming on the rough, choppy sea. "Snow?" he asks.

Troy shakes his head. "Water. Salt water, to be precise. It covers approximately three-quarters of the earth."

"Snow is all white," Pippa says. "White and cold and soft as a feather when it touches your skin."

"Oh," Googol says sadly. "We don't have any skin."

Suddenly, the two robots think that ugly human bodies might be good for something, after all.

"Look!" Troy points towards the horizon. There, in front of them, is a glimmer of white. "Snow!"

A few moments later, they are flying over snowy hills and white plateaus. Googol steers them towards a nice sharp point and parks the ship. Troy is just about to point out that this might not be such a good parking spot when the spaceship begins to slide. Like a big toboggan, it coasts right down the side of the hill.

"Whoa!" Troy yells.

"Whee!" Pippa cries.

The spaceship comes slowly to a stop as it plows onto a flat piece of ice.

"Oh my!" Googolplex says. Lights flash all over his body and his head spins around three times.

"That was fun!" Googol says.

"Yes, sledding is my favorite thing to do in winter time. We do it on a hill near our house as soon as it snows," Pippa says.

"Lucky humans!" Googol and Googolplex say at the same time.

The robots think they are going to like this stuff called snow.

Chapter Three
Snow-bots

Pippa is glad that they have brought their winter clothes with them. The air outside the spaceship is so cold that her nose feels like an ice crystal. And she would probably slip on the icy ground if she didn't have her boots on.

The robots don't worry about such things. They roll right out of the spaceship onto the snow just as they are. After all, they can't feel the cold. Their bodies are perfect for any weather. At least, that's what they think until their wheels touch the ground and slide right out from under them.

Thump! Right on their backs they go. First Googol falls, then Googolplex. Troy and Pippa try

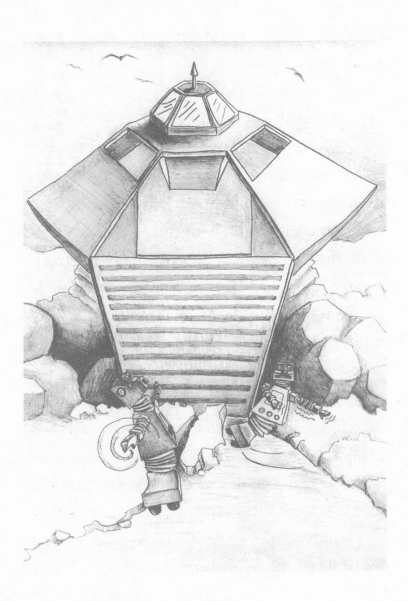

not to laugh, but it's hard not to. The robots look so funny lying in the snow.

"How embarrassing," Googol says.

"We should have retracted our super-retractable self-adhesive wheels," says Googolplex.

"We should have," Googol agrees. "Our wheels don't appear to stick to snow."

"Well, while you're down there, you may as well make the most of it," Pippa says. She collapses on her back beside them and starts to flap her arms and legs up and down along the top of the snow. "Do this."

The robots turn their heads to watch her.

"I don't think we can do that," Googol says.

Their feet move up and down only a little, but both robots manage to slide their arms in the snow.

Pippa rolls carefully up from the snow. Then she and Troy take the robots' arms and pull them to their feet.

"Up you go!" Troy says.

Troy and Pippa wipe the snow off the robots' backs. Then they turn them about.

Pippa points down at the pictures they have made in the snow. "Snow angels," she says.

"Snow-bots," Troy says with a laugh. And sure enough, the pictures of Googol and Googolplex look more like robots with wings than angels. They have left all of their nice sharp lines and corners pressed into the snow.

"Perfect," Googol says.

"Perfect," Googolplex says. "May we keep them?"

"I shouldn't think so," Troy says. "Every snow angel I've ever made has been snowed under or washed away."

Googolplex gives a long, sad beep. "How sad."

"How very, very sad," Googol says.

Pippa lifts her face and catches a snowflake on her tongue. "Look! It's snowing!"

Troy leaps forward and squashes some snow together between his mittens. He holds it up to show the robots.

"A snowball," Troy says. Then he curls his

hand around the ball of snow and throws it at his sister.

Pippa screams and drops to her knees to make her own snowball. She throws it at Troy, and he throws another one back at her.

"What are you doing?" Googol asks. His head spins around three times when one of Pippa's snowballs hits him right in the nose.

"Oops! Sorry about that, Googol," Pippa says.

"We're having a snowball fight!" Troy says. "That's what snowballs are for."

"That, and making snowmen," Pippa says.

"How odd. How very odd," Googol says as the snow drips from his face.

"What is a snowman?" Googolplex asks.

"We'll show you," Troy says.

Troy and Pippa roll three different size balls and pile them up. Pippa points to the head.

"There should be two buttons for eyes, and a carrot for a nose," Pippa says.

Googol and Googolplex stare at the snowman in silence. Then they make a series of squeaks and beeps.

"I like him," Googolplex says.

"Could you make a square one?" Googol asks.

Troy and Pippa exchange glances.

"It would be very hard to roll squares," Pippa says.

"We could cut square blocks out of the snow bank if we had a knife," Troy says.

Googol beeps excitedly. "Next time we will bring a knife."

Googolplex leans down and packs a small snowball together. "For now, this will have to do."

Googolplex opens a small compartment in his chest and places three snowballs inside. Googol does the same thing.

"Now, I think it might be time for us to take you home," Googol says. "I think the father-who-is-not-king might come out of his study soon."

Chapter Four
Lost and Found

This time, the robots land their spaceship on the Sinclairs' lawn. Pippa and Troy step out onto the grass and sniff the air.

"The neighbors are having roast chicken tonight," Troy says.

Pippa smacks her lips. "I can just about taste it!"

"What is this 'taste'?" Googolplex asks.

"It's how sweet or sour, or how delicious, something is when you put it into your mouth and eat it," Troy says.

Googol and Googolplex look at each other. "Eat?"

"You don't eat? Huh." Troy shakes his head.

"How do you get your energy, then?"

"Solar energy from our Sunship gives our spaceship energy, and our spaceship gives us energy," Googolplex answers.

"Every night, we must sit in our cockpit and recharge ourselves, or we stop working," Googol says.

"But then, why did you want a chocolate bar?" Pippa asks.

"You're suppose to eat it," Troy explains.

Googolplex spins his head around three times. "Oh, dear. Does it taste good?"

"Wonderful!" Pippa says. "It's sweet and chocolate-y and, oooh, so delicious that it's impossible to describe!"

"Oh, dear," Googol says. "Another thing you humans can do that we can't!"

"How distressing," Googolplex says.

Troy smiles. "Yeah, being an ugly human isn't so bad, is it, Pip?"

Pippa smiles at him. "Nope. It's pretty darn good most of the time. But you know, Googolplex, I think it's pretty neat to be a robot too."

"Do you?" Googolplex asks.

"Do you?" Googol asks.

"We sure do," Troy answers. "And tomorrow we'll help you find some more things on your list, if you like."

"We like!" Googolplex says.

"We like very much," Googol says.

Troy and Pippa laugh and run towards the house.

"See you tomorrow, then," they call back to the robots.

The next day is Saturday, and it's cleaning day at the Sinclairs' house. Troy and Pippa help by vacuuming and dusting. When they're done, they hang around the family room waiting for the robots. But Googol and Googolplex don't appear.

"What do you think has happened to them?" Pippa asks her brother.

"I don't know. Maybe they had to go back to their Sunship," Troy answers.

Mr. Sinclair shows up with a basket of laundry. He tells Troy and Pippa that if they're finished their chores they can go outside to play until lunchtime.

Pippa drags her feet on the way out.

"I don't understand it. They said they'd be here," she says.

"They'll be back. Don't worry," Troy says.

"There's no way they can find all those things on their list without our help."

Troy picks up a Frisbee from the front lawn and tosses it across to Pippa.

"Catch!" he yells.

But before Pippa has a chance to, the Frisbee bounces strangely in the air and crashes to the ground. Pippa and Troy look at each other, then they both run into the middle of the lawn. They stop as they near the area where the Frisbee has landed.

"Do you think it's still here?" Pippa asks.

"It must be." Troy feels carefully through the air with his arms outstretched. He walks forward inch by inch until his legs jam up against something. "Aha!"

Pippa rushes in and slides her hands against the robot's invisible spaceship. Her fingers latch onto something.

"I think it's the door!" she says. She pushes

a button and the ramp drops down in front of them. Now they can see right inside the spaceship.

Troy and Pippa walk up the ramp into the spaceship.

"Googol?" they call. "Googolplex!"

But the inside of the spaceship is empty. The robots are not in their cockpit or anywhere else.

Troy scratches his head.

"I don't like it," he says. "If the robots' spaceship is here, Googol and Googolplex should be around somewhere too."

"Look!" Pippa says.

She points out one of the side windows of the spaceship. Troy squints hard. He finally sees a little bit of blue, red and yellow sticking out of the long grass at the back of their house.

Troy and Pippa run out of the spaceship and into their back yard. They find both robots lying in the grass under a very big apple tree.

Pippa laughs. "What are you guys doing? Counting the apples?"

The robots don't answer. They just lie there, staring up at the sky.

"Oh, no!" Troy says. He kneels down beside Googol and stares into the robot's dull eyes. "They're out of power!"

And Troy is right. There isn't a single light flashing from any part of the robots' bodies. They have stopped working.

Chapter Five
Martin Kelly

Pippa stands and stares down at Googol and Googolplex. She feels like crying.

"What are we going to do, Troy?" she asks.

"We're going to get them back to their spaceship and recharge them, that's what we're going to do!" Troy says. "Go get your red wagon, Pippa!"

Pippa runs to get her wagon from the back porch. It squeaks noisily as she wheels it over to her brother.

Troy and Pippa lift Googol and lay him in the wagon. The robot is smaller than Pippa and he isn't much heavier than an empty garbage can. Pippa and Troy don't have much trouble pulling him over to the spaceship and up the ramp. Putting Googol into his cockpit and hooking him up to be recharged is trickier. They've never had to plug in a robot before.

Pippa finally sees the two slots in the floor underneath the cockpit. When they roll Googol backwards his feet fit perfectly into these slots. After only ten seconds, all Googol's lights flash on and his head turns around three times.

"Oh, dear!" Googol exclaims. "Oh, dear, dear, dear, dear, dear! That was an awful experience. That was a terrible experience!"

Pippa puts a hand on top of Googol's head. "Take it easy, Googol. You're okay."

"What happened?" Troy asks.

"We heard a blackbird's song," Googol says, sadly.

"And?" Troy says.

"And it was so beautiful!" Googol says. "It's on our list, you know."

"I know, I know," Troy says, "but what has that got to do with you and Googolplex being out of power?"

Just then, Troy looks into their back yard. A couple of blackbirds land in the apple tree.

"You didn't try to climb our tree and catch a blackbird, did you?" Troy asks.

Googol nods.

"Oh, Googol! You silly robot!" Troy says.

"Yes, very silly," Googol agrees. "The blackbirds flew away and left us, and we couldn't get down. We ran out of power when your sun was rising, and I guess we fell."

"You poor thing!" Pippa exclaims.

Troy looks Googol over, but the robot doesn't have a scratch on him.

"Could you bring Googolplex back to the spaceship too?" Googol asks. "I don't like to see him lying there all alone."

Troy and Pippa run back to Googolplex and load him into the wagon. But just as they begin to pull him towards the spaceship, they see Martin Kelly walking over from next door.

"Oh, no!" Troy whispers to Pippa.

Martin is two years older than Troy and a bit of a bully. On a good day when he has friends over to play with, he ignores Pippa and Troy completely. But on a bad day when he is bored, he hangs their toys in the trees and shoots spitballs at them. Pippa and Troy know Googol and Googolplex will be in trouble if Martin finds out about them.

Pippa and Troy stand in front of the wagon and try to hide Googolplex. But they can tell by the way that Martin starts to run towards them that he has seen the robot.

"What have you got there?" Martin asks.

"It's just a robot," Troy says.

"Does it work?" Martin asks. He makes a grab for Googolplex, but Pippa pulls the wagon away.

"No," Troy says.

Pippa keeps walking towards the invisible spaceship and Martin keeps following.

"Come on. Let's see him stand up," Martin says.

Just then, Troy realizes that the spaceship ramp is still down. If they take one more step, Martin will be able to see right up inside the spaceship.

"All right, Martin. But you have to close your eyes and count to thirty," Troy says. "And no cheating!"

Martin grumbles a lot, but he finally puts a hand over his eyes and starts counting.

Troy grabs Pippa's hand and leads her quickly up the spaceship's ramp. By the time Martin starts peeking through his fingers, the ramp has closed. Now Troy and Pippa are invisible too.

Martin pulls his hand right away from his face. "Hey! Where'd you guys go?"

Pippa and Troy stand in front of the spaceship windows. They watch Martin turn around and around, looking for them.

"Uh-oh," Pippa says. "Watch out! He's going to bump into us."

Martin has made himself so dizzy spinning around that he walks right into the side of the spaceship. He rubs his head. Then he puts out a hand and walks towards them.

"Hold on!" Googol calls.

Pippa and Troy hold onto a wall as Googol makes the spaceship lift off and hover above Martin's head. Martin stands under them, swatting the air and charging around like a mad bull.

Googol and Googolplex are so busy escaping from Martin that they forget all about falling out of the apple tree. And when Pippa and Troy hear the robots bleeping happily once again, they are almost glad to have someone as silly as Martin Kelly for a neighbor.

Chapter Six
The Blackbird's Song

Martin is still running around under the robots' invisible spaceship when Mr. Sinclair comes out of the house.

"Here comes Dad," Pippa says.

Martin runs over to Mr. Sinclair as soon as he sees him. Mr. Sinclair scratches his head as if he can't understand a thing Martin is saying.

"Googol, you'd better drop us off at the back of the house," Troy says.

"Before Martin gets us in too much trouble," Pippa says.

In a couple of minutes, Troy and Pippa come running around to the front of the house. Mr. Sinclair points to them as soon as he sees them.

"See? There they are, Martin," Mr. Sinclair says. "Nothing can disappear into thin air, you know."

"Yeah?" Martin says angrily. He looks down into Pippa's empty wagon. "Well, where's the robot then?"

"Gone, I'm afraid," Troy says.

Martin sticks his chin out. "You promised that I could see him!"

Troy nods. "I know. But he's rather shy of people, and I can't make him do something he doesn't want to."

"You're lying!" Martin waves hands about. "He's here, somewhere, flying about. And I have the bump on my head to prove it!"

Mr. Sinclair rolls his eyes. "Martin, go home and have some lunch. A person can't think clearly on an empty stomach."

Martin looks like he's about to argue with Mr. Sinclair again, but he doesn't. He turns around and stamps all the way home.

Mr. Sinclair shakes his head. "I don't know what gets into that boy sometimes."

Mr. Sinclair looks over at his own children.

"So," Mr. Sinclair says, "where is this robot?"

"He's in the back yard in his invisible spaceship," Troy says.

"He's being recharged," Pippa says.

Mr. Sinclair laughs and pats Pippa's head. "Good for him. Now how about I go in and make some lunch to recharge the rest of us? Tuna fish okay?"

"Sure, Dad," Pippa says.

"Sure, Dad," Troy says.

As soon as Mr. Sinclair has gone inside the house, Troy and Pippa run back to the spaceship to see the robots.

"How are you doing?" Troy asks the robots. "Are you all recharged?"

"Oh, no. That will take us the rest of the day," Googolplex says.

"The blackbirds will probably be gone by then," Googol says sadly.

"No they won't," Pippa says. "They're always here."

"Are they? Oh, you're so lucky," Googol says.

"We don't have anything that makes a song half as nice as that back on our Sunship."

"I'm not going to mind having to sit here all day being recharged as long as I can listen to the blackbirds," Googolplex says. "If only we could catch one for our scavenger hunt."

"Oh, you can't do that," Troy says. "The blackbirds need to stay in their own environment here on earth to survive."

"Anyway," Pippa says, "your list didn't say to get a blackbird, it said to get a blackbird's song. And I think I know how to do that."

"You do?" Googol and Googolplex say together.

Pippa laughs. "Yes. But you'll have to wait till later, because my dad is taking us swimming after lunch."

"Is your dad mad at you for helping us?" Googol asked them.

"Oh, no," Pippa says. "He doesn't believe you're real."

"Not real!" Googolplex exclaims.

"Not real!" Googol exclaims. He gives three very real beeps.

"Don't worry about it," Troy says. "It's better if we keep you a secret, anyway. A lot of adults would want to lock you up and take you apart if they found you. They're very scared of the idea of creatures coming here from outer space."

"Yeah, and it's a good thing you didn't go down Martin's chimney," Pippa says. "He'd probably have locked you in his basement and made the neighborhood kids pay to see you."

"Oh, dear!" Googol says. "I don't think we will go down any more chimneys!"

"And I don't think I want to meet any adults!" Googolplex says.

"We'll just stay right here while we recharge," Googol says.

And Googol and Googolplex have a very nice afternoon listening to the blackbirds in the apple tree—until Martin Kelly returns.

Chapter Seven
Falling Snowballs

Googol and Googolplex are still sitting in their cockpit listening to the blackbirds when Martin Kelly climbs over the side fence into the Sinclairs' back yard. The robots watch him sneak over to the Sinclairs' apple tree with a couple of stones in his hand.

"Oh, dear," Googol says.

"Oh, dear," Googolplex says.

Martin pulls back his arm and throws the stones high into the tree. All the blackbirds fly away. Martin laughs.

"That Martin Kelly!" Googol says.

"He is not a very nice human!" Googolplex says.

Martin reaches up into the apple tree and starts to climb it. He is a very good climber. It takes him only a couple of minutes to reach the very top of the tree. The robots can barely see him through the leaves. When Pippa comes out of the house into the back yard, she does not see Martin at all.

Pippa has a small blue and white tape recorder in her hand. It is the one her father bought her for Christmas. She carries it over to the apple tree and puts it down on the ground. She pushes the record button.

"Pippa!" Mr. Sinclair calls from the back porch. "The popcorn's ready!"

"Coming, Dad!" Pippa calls back.

Pippa turns and smiles in the direction of the robot's invisible spaceship. She gives them a little wave before she runs back into the house.

Martin sticks his head out through the leaves of the apple tree to see if the coast is clear.

"I do not like the look of this," Googolplex says. "That Martin Kelly is up to no good."

And Googolplex is right. As soon as Martin climbs down out of the tree, he grabs Pippa's tape recorder and runs away with it.

"No! Stop!" Googol yells.

"Bring that back!" Googolplex yells.

But Martin can't see or hear the robots. He puts Pippa's tape recorder under one arm and keeps running until he is back in his own yard.

"We must get Pippa's little box back," Googol says.

"Yes," Googolplex agrees. "It is her box. I do not think she would want Martin Kelly to have it."

The robots push a few buttons that make the spaceship fly up and over to the Kellys' back yard. They see Martin hiding behind a playhouse. He is pushing the buttons on Pippa's tape recorder and making strange noises.

"How are we going to get it back if we can't leave the spaceship?" Googol asks Googolplex.

"I do not know," Googolplex answers. "I do not want to be locked up in Martin Kelly's basement."

"Neither do I," Googol says. "But Pippa and Troy have helped us and we must help them. We could not have found a chocolate bar and snowballs without them."

Googolplex's head spins around three times. "That is it, Googol! The snowballs!"

Martin is still sitting on the grass. He is growling and burping and yelling rude words onto Pippa's tape. He doesn't know anything is going to happen to him until the first snowball drops onto the top of his head.

Martin stumbles onto his feet and looks up at the sunny blue sky. "What the heck?" he says.

Martin falls back onto his knees and covers his head as five more snowballs fly out of the sky at him. When they stop, Martin gets to his feet and runs into his house.

"Mom! Mom!" Martin yells as the back door crashes closed behind him.

"Oh, that felt good!" Googol says.

"Wonderful!" Googolplex says. "I like snowball fights! I think we should tell all the robots on our Sunship to have one as soon as we get back!"

"Good idea!" Googol says. "But right now I think we had better grab Pippa's box and go!"

Googol hits a button on the spaceship's control panel. A little door beneath the spaceship opens and out pops a robotic arm. Googol guides this arm down to Pippa's tape recorder and makes it grab hold of the blue handle.

Googolplex flies the spaceship back into the Sinclairs' back yard. The robotic arm gently replaces Pippa's tape recorder under the apple tree.

"Perfect!" Googolplex says.

"Perfect!" Googol says.

By the time Martin Kelly drags his mother out of the house, there is nothing to see. No robotic arm, no tape recorder and no snowballs. The warm spring sun has melted the snowballs into puddles on the grass.

"Poor Martin Kelly," Googolplex says. "He is not having a good day."

"No," Googol says. "But we are!"

"We certainly are!" Googolplex says.

And the robots' lights flash like laughter as they listen to Martin try to convince his mother that there really were snowballs falling on him out of the warm blue sky.

Chapter Eight
Shooting Stars and Sunships

The next morning, Troy and Pippa take the tape recorder up into the robots' spaceship. Googol and Googolplex quickly tell them all about their adventures with Martin Kelly. When they play back the tape in the tape recorder, they find everything the robots have told them is taped on it. They hear all of Martin's rude words. They hear the snowball attack. And they hear Martin trying to convince his mother that snowballs are falling out of the blue sky.

Pippa and Troy shake their heads.

"Well, at least things turned out all right in the end," Pippa says.

And they really did, because the second half of Pippa's tape is filled with the blackbirds' songs.

"Perfect!" Googol says.

"Perfect!" Googolplex says.

"Now all we have to figure out is how you are going to be able to listen to this tape if you take it back to your Sunship," Pippa says. "I suppose I could loan you my tape recorder…"

"Thank you, Pippa, but you don't need to," Googolplex tells her. "Our spaceship has a sound recorder too."

"If we play your tape again, we can record it into the memory banks of our computer," Googol says.

"Okay, but remember not to record Martin Kelly's part," Troy reminds them. "We don't want the robots on your Sunship to think that all humans sound like that. They'll blast out of our solar system for sure."

They all laugh.

Once the blackbirds' songs have been safely stored on their spaceship's memory banks, Googol hands back Pippa's tape recorder.

"Thank you. Now I think we must go back to our Sunship," Googol tells her.

"Must you?" Troy asks. "You haven't got half the things on your list yet."

"And you used up all your snowballs," Pippa reminds them.

"That is true," Googol says. "We will have to stop at the North Pole on the way home and get some more."

Pippa and Troy are very sad when they realize that the robots really mean to leave.

"Don't worry," Googolplex tells them. "Our scavenger hunt is not over. We are just going home to recharge our spaceship. Then we will be back."

"Soon?" Troy asks.

"Oh, very soon," Googolple says. "It doesn't take too many of your earth hours to get to our Sunship and back again."

"I wish we could go with you," Pippa says.

"I think the father-who-is-not-king would miss you," Googol says.

"I think he would too," Troy agrees. But Troy still dreams about how incredible it would be someday to visit the robot's Sunship.

"Good-bye, then," Troy says, as the robots drop the ramp door to let them out of their spaceship.

"Hold on! I've got to give you something before you go!" Pippa says.

She runs back to her house. When she comes back she is carrying a bread and butter knife. "So you can make a square snowman!"

Googol carefully puts the knife into the compartment in his chest. "Oh, thank you! We will have a great time at the North Pole now!"

"Just remember to retract your wheels this time," Troy tells them.

"We will!" Googol promises.

"We will!" Googolplex promises. And then they are off.

Troy and Pippa wave for a few moments at the empty blue sky. Then they walk slowly back to the house.

"What do you imagine a square snowman will look like?" Troy asks Pippa.

"All lovely and smooth with lots of sharp corners and edges, I imagine," Pippa says. "Just like Googol and Googolplex."

That night, Pippa and Troy look out of their bedroom window and watch for shooting stars.

"You haven't seen any, have you?" Troy asks Pippa.

"Not one," Pippa answers.

Troy sighs. "I wish I knew where they were right now."

They snuggle down in their beds to go to sleep.

"I'm sure glad Googol and Googolplex decided to come down our chimney," Pippa says sleepily.

"Me too," Troy says.

"I hope Santa Claus doesn't mind someone else using it," Pippa says.

Troy laughs. "I don't think he will, as long as Googol and Googolplex don't get in his way on Christmas Eve. Now go to sleep."

That night, while Troy and Pippa lie sleeping, a tiny star shoots across the sky and stops above the earth to shine even more brightly upon it than it did before. And from somewhere far, far away comes the song of a blackbird.

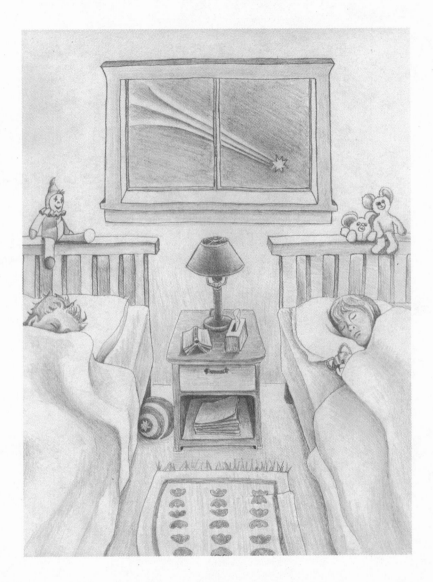

Nelly Kazenbroot is a published poet, a lyricist and an artist. When her children were younger, she built two tiny robots from Lego, gave them silly voices and characteristics and named them Googol and Googolplex. Now her characters live in print. She lives in Nanaimo, British Columbia.